AF455158

# “LIGHT TRAVELERS”

BY
DAWN NELLIS


ISBN-10: 0557744539
ISBN-13: 978-0557744534

Published in the United States of America

# LIGHT TRAVELERS

The tri-sunned sky was cloudless over the lush oasis. Theta, the smallest star, would be burning out soon – several months, maybe sooner – and a black hole would be born. Time shift. It was a dark orange against its sister sun's, Mu, bright blue. Omega, the largest and youngest, beamed yellow.

Linea gazed into the sky leaning on the threshold of the mud and rock abode, naked, taking in the heat of the suns. On this part of the planet was always daylight longer. The rays from the suns browned their skin. She and her husband, Cali, were the only inhabitants of this fertile shelter in the midst of rocky dunes.

She glanced over her shoulder. Cali still slept, but stirred restlessly. Love gleamed in her eyes. Linea watched him for a few moments. His long lean body lay sprawled across their sleeping platform. His muscular limbs were gracefully in sight while the tanned animal hides hid Cali's lithe torso. Sunlight sparkled in his thick golden brown hair. The locks fell over into his handsome face. There was a sly smile on his face that made her wonder what were in his dreams. Slowly, rays of the first sun struck his eyelids; Cali turned onto his side and buried his head under the skins. Linea silently went to him and carefully pulled the coverings from over his head.

She whispered in his ear, "Whom do you love?"

"Linea," he answered in his slumber and began to lightly snore.

Satisfied with his answer, the young woman strolled around the structure to a lonely waterfall streaming from an overhanging semicircle of rocky ledges. It faced away from the suns, but the water was still very warm. Linea brought the liquid to her face and thought of her duties for the day. First, she must prepare Cali's meal.

With fish impaled on a spear, she noisily moved around the cooking area. Cali slyly watched her bouncing around in a thong and short tunic. A short blade strapped to her right thigh. He slowly sat up in the large feather and down bed. He pushed the fiber woven covers and fur coverlets aside, wiping the sleep from his eyes. He stretched and yawned.

Fish began frying on an oiled flat rock in the center of the fire.

"Good morning."

"Finally, you've waken," she continued to cook, "I have your meal. You should be hungry since you slept late."

He jumped from the bed and quickly arranged the covers neatly, "How late is it?"

"Already Mu sets, but you could be early by Omega. Theta is in midday." She was chopping vegetables and mixing them onto the fish. Cali was not listening – he was watching her prance about; her long black hair in a braid swinging at her back. He sighed and straightened.

"Are you well?" he finally heard, "did you not hear me, Cali?"

Linea turned and looked at him.

"What did you say, my love?" he asked sarcastically. She laughed as he came toward her.

"Oh no, I have already bathed. You are being…" A shriek exploded from her lips as Cali lifted her and lain her on their hide covered bed. His lips covered hers. Strong hands caressed the soft skin.

He whispered in her ear, "I am being…what?"

"Slow, Cali, extremely slow."

She pulled on a pair of chaps, leaving Cali to chronicle his observations of their world. Linea promised him she would return before Omega set.

Grabbing a satchel, she strode into the dunes until she came upon a field of sun dried grasses. She took a long deep breath and let out a long, sweet one-note song. The sound echoed and picked up a harmony. A great roar returned and echoed. The woman scanned the sky and focused on a red creature in flight on the horizon. The creature became larger and larger as it approached. Its massive body shadowed her as its great wings fanned the grasses flat around Linea. The dragon slowly and gently landed in front of her, bowing its head for a petting.

"Oh great Sula," Linea said into the dragon's ear, "How beautiful you become every time I see you. And so big!" She pets the scaly beast's neck. Its rough skin reflected gold and silver iridescence from the bright sky, his wings folded neatly on its sides. Sula's blue eyes winked at Linea.

She bowed to him, "Sula, will you take me to the bountiful fields?"

The great reptile raises its crowned head and crouched to let Linea mount him. She grabbed up her satchel and scrambled atop Sula. With a loving tap on his neck from Linea, Sula spread his magnificent wings and took off into the sky.

Cali watched them from his window as they soared away. They glided far across the sky, Linea laughing as the wind whipped past her, far past the perimeter of the lea where their home lies.

He wondered if he should have called her back. The time was due. In the corner of his room stood his staff carved from an ancient petrified mahogany, floating above the staff was a crystal orb the size of an eye. And as Linea traveled further and further away the orb glowed brighter and brighter.

Cali continued to write. Waiting was always difficult. But it had to be done.

Scanning the white sea and pink sands, the green prairie and dense forests, Linea took in the beauty of her home, and it was all theirs. She and Cali's. She sighed. Was it right to be so happy?

After gathering enough foodstuffs, Sula and Linea rested. They were just inside the small area of the earth where the darkness prevailed away from the heat of the suns. They could see into the light that was just a short walk away. The red dragon lay peacefully as she reclined on the creature's warm side. The warmth from Sula and the suns a short distance away lulled Linea to sleep.

She heard Cali's voice; it was faint and unclear. His face emerged from the darkness. He looked alarmed. Linea called to him in her slumber.

She woke with a start. Linea rose alertly and unsheathed her blade. Omega was in early evening and the only sun in the sky. She was not alarmed because of the time or her dream, but Sula was crouched, ready to flame with a growl deep in his throat. His tongue flickered through his enormous jagged teeth. He stood agitated toward the darkened east. Whatever alarmed him was between them and home. Linea cautiously stepped to view what had Sula's attention.

"I have come, Linea," a deep, rich voice called out. A large man was far away, strolling closer. He stepped into the darkness. Above him, an orb lit up his way. He wore a long black hooded tunic; his eyes were white as his hair, eyebrows and lashes. His right hand was across his chest, his skin as black as his robe. On his pointing finger was a golden snake-shaped ring, with jade eyes and ruby tongue. The man smiles when Linea was in view from behind the dragon.

"Who are you? How do you know me?" Linea had never seen another person on their earth. And she felt there was no one else necessary. She didn't know why she felt that way. It always was. But this man seemed familiar.

"I am Lord Uomo," he said incredulously and stopped walking towards the girl and the dragon, "your master."

"Ha, I have only one master and he does not rule me but I serve him. You are nothing to us, Lord Uomo. Leave as you came. Leave us be!"

Lord Uomo began walking again, his pace quicker with a laugh in his throat.

"We are from an ancient time. You, Cali and I. Gods hath betrothed you to Cali when I am the one who rightfully holds your destiny. Ask Cali. He knows the truth."

"Truth to what? Your desires mean nothing to me. My desires are nothing to you. Go back from where you came, Uomo. You are not wanted here. Hear me and beware."

Suddenly he was upon her, grabbing her arm that held the blade. Her feet were off the ground as he looked into her eyes. Sula could do nothing but roar; if he flamed, he would also burn Linea.

"I am your desire, Linea." His touch seared.

The blade fell from her right hand into the left.

"You arrogant swine!" She plunged the blade into his neck. He dropped her, and the girl scrambled away. Uomo's big hand wrapped around the handle of the blade and pulled it from his neck. The weapon then melted in his ringed hand. There was no wound, no blood. Linea, in disbelief, was riveted to her hiding place behind Sula. He came toward her again.

Sula spat at him, setting Uomo afire.

"Linea, calm your pet. I do not wish to hurt him. Calm him and come with me."

The flames were no more. His cape was neither singed nor smoldering. Afraid, Linea jumped onto Sula's back and urged him to fly.

"I would rather die."

Sula took flight. Linea did not look back to Uomo who thrice clapped his large hands causing an ill wind. The dragon screeched in pain. Tears filled Linea eyes as she watched

Sula's flesh and blood crystallize beneath her. Through the glass dragon she saw Uomo.

Tears blinded her, "Sula…"

They were falling. She tried her best to hold onto the dragon and thought about Cali. Why was this happening? Linea wanted to die rather than live with Uomo and without her love, Cali. Her death came closer. The ground quickly met her.

Cali stopped waiting and summoned his staff. It floated, zipping to his open palm. The orb's light became intense as he carried it outside. He stabbed the staff into the earth and knelt in front of it. Arms outstretched in front around the staff, the orb lit up the early evening. Cali knew Uomo would block their energies. So, Cali began to track Linea's lifelight. He spoke though his lips did not move.

"Lifelight, take me to her!"

Linea opened her eyes, her face in the lush grass, and turned her head. A wall of shattered crystal lay around her. There was no pain. She felt groggy.

"Cali," she whispered as she was lifted. But all she saw was Uomo's black face through dazed eyes. His blue eyes did not disguise victory. Victory over what? Linea tried to struggle, but she could not move.

"Why, where are you taking me?"

She saw black.

It was cold.

It was damp.

Linea shivered. Her shock to the coolness forced her to awareness. She sprung into a corner as her eyes began adjusting to the darkness. She had no idea where she was.

"You are awake. Good," she heard Uomo say. Linea could only see his glowing eyes coming toward her. The closer he came, the less they glowed. She reached for her sheath and remembered the blade was gone. *How I can protect myself against a mystic?* she thought.

"Do not come near my presence, Lord Uomo."

She heard him laugh quietly deep in his chest. He mused that this moment happened again and again for over a millennia. And now, finally, she was his.

"My lovely Linea, this is my domain and here I do what pleases me."

She saw the golden ring sway. The vast room became lit. There were no window or doors. The source of light came from the only thing in the room: a four-poster bed. Above the golden posts hovered glowing orbs. Coiled directly under the orbs atop the posts were snakes, the same as Uomo's ring. They grinned hideously at her.

"I see what you want, Uomo. I am not yours to take."

"I will take you whether you are mine or not. Then you will be mine nevertheless!"

Linea stood and ran at him, "Then you will fight for it!"

"Nonsense, but quaint." He waved his ringed hand again. The snakes from the posts slithered down and wrapped themselves around her arms and legs. Linea quickly tried to pull them off. Uomo pointed to the wall behind her and she was slammed against it. The snakes coiled themselves tightly up and down her limbs. Their tiny heads lay on her shoulders and hips, tongues flickering. The more she struggled, the more strength they absorbed, holding her securely against the wall. Uomo's eyes began to glow again. Linea's garments fell from her. Naked, she shivered from the cold and Uomo's lustful stare. His hot finger touched her lips. She tried to bite him, but the finger made a path down her neck, between her breasts.

"Let me make you more powerful. A woman. Come to me, accept me. Cali can do nothing for you." Her body arched unwilling toward Uomo. She could not fight him.

"We are destined to be together, Linea."

"Never," she said as she tried to free herself, "never!"

Uomo sighed and opened his robe and let it drop to the floor. His bare muscular body shone in the dim light taut and ready with desire.

"So be it."

His arms circled her waist. His chest upon her breast. The heat from his body burned her. She screamed.

Cali materialized.

"Stop Uomo," he tapped his staff against the floor. A blast of light struck Uomo crashing him away from Linea. Linea, in a trance, dropped her head back. Uomo grabbed his robe, pulling it on while standing between Cali and Linea.

"She is mine, Cali," he growled.

Cali was calm. "You cannot have her. She is a power of her own design that cannot be controlled. And you know it. What will you gain taking it by force?"

"She has the power and does not even know of it. With me it will flourish."

"Move, Uomo. Let her be. Why must we argue time after time over something you cannot possess and corrupt?"

"I will have her even if I have to kill you."

"Like you did the dragon? That is why you'll never have anything. You kill what others love. You have no compassion, no love. Something Linea is all of. Someone you will never, ever have."

Uomo's ringed hand opened upward. The poster bed orbs lifted and merged into one turning into a black crystal. It then sped past Cali's head to hover over Uomo's palm.

"Don't Uomo. You won't gain until you learn." Cali's orb emanated a light blanching the stone room white, "Listen to me, damn you!"

The black orb blasted a beam at Cali. It seeped through the brightness. As the dark beam edged closer to Cali, the room became darker. The earth quaked and a high-pitched scream echoed in the room. His black crystal weakened. Cali's crystal grew brighter. Both ethereal men looked toward the sound.

Linea's hair flared about her head with static electricity flickering and crackling loudly. Her eyes fluttered, then opened and rays of light streamed from them into Cali's orb and Uomo's crystal. The crystal turned emanated a rainbow of colors then white and the orb became ever brighter. Uomo dropped the precious stone and cursed it. He cursed Cali; he dared not curse Linea.

"No Linea…" Uomo moved away, stunned.

Linea spoke to him in a trance, "Your time will come."

The snakes vaporized from her limbs. Linea feet gently met the stone floor.

"Come," Cali held his hand out for her. She became clothed in a flowing white gown as her hand gently grasped his in her blindness. The earth's tremors increased, "the time distortion opens."

Their energies glowed and melded until there was only a column of light that disappeared into the walls of the room, leaving Uomo alone and raving.

# PRESENT – SPRINGTIME

She was up before the alarm went off. For an hour, she watched her husband sleep restlessly. A tiny smile was on his lips that created the dimples that made Cali so sexy. Was his reverie as weird and wonderful as hers, she wondered. The strangest dream…

Now at 6:24 A.M., one minute before the alarm, she caressed his body to wake him. Linea wanted to make sure his day started off right.

"Do you have to go to the office today? Can't you work from home?" He later asked her.

She looked at him in the mirror as she applied her lipstick, "I could. Only if you really want me to."

"I do. I really do."

"Alright," she went over to kiss him, "but I need some papers. I'll be right back."

"Do you know that I love you?"

She laughed, "It's as bright as three suns." Cali looked at Linea. She doesn't remember; it was a coincidence. He hugged her and didn't let go.

"Hey, I will be right back."

He forced himself to free her, "I know." She smiled dazzlingly and walked out of the room jangling her cars keys on her finger. She called back.

"When are you going to finish your book?"

"Don't know. Maybe soon. My publisher's bugging me." He leaned on the threshold, watching her descend the stairs.

"Want me to talk to him? I don't want my baby stressed."

"Nah, I'm ignoring him."

"Ha!" He heard the front door close, the car rev up shortly after and speed off down the street. When he was sure she was gone, Cali went into the bathroom and turned on the shower. He let it run hot. It was almost like the waterfalls back… Well, almost. He turned on the radio. He liked music, especially jazz and classical instrumental. Rock and rap was noisy and pop just didn't cut it. Though at times rhythm and blues moved him, as did soul.

Cali liked the gadgets and inventions of this time. It secretly took him two years to adapt to this new world of cars, microwave ovens and computers. Linea was prepared, while in their auras during the time bending. They were protected from Uomo who continually blasted into their energies to no avail. Theta burned out, Uomo got stronger, but they escaped unharmed. Cali knew Uomo would follow sooner or later; he was determined to have Linea. The destruction of Cali would the exact of Linea. Uomo would never understand. Never.

Cali stepped into the shower. The steamy cascade eased his tensions. He feared that in this time Uomo could win what he desired. He wasn't afraid for himself, only for Linea. The twenty-second century was almost upon them. A very turbulent period told to him by the orb.

After his shower, Cali dressed in a long tunic, a gift from Linea. He disliked pants in the summer. He disliked underwear even more though they kept everything from bouncing around. Like brassieres. He hated when Linea strapped herself into that contraption, though they did make her look real nice. Alas, this is what man called modern. He went downstairs, into the kitchen. Cali poured hand-squeezed orange juice from a glass pitcher; coated paper containers made the juice flavor of the juice taste artificial. The kitchen was the only place where he was pleased with technology: wood burning stove fireplace in the corner of the room, a generous double sink, fully stocked pantry and refrigerator and extra wide tables to work and eat on.

And there were lights everywhere. For everything. Modern man could not do without his own inventions.

In the study, Cali sat before his computer. Filled with books, magazines and newspapers of every kind in every language from all over the world scattered in messy but organized stacks, but he knew where each piece lay if he had to refer to it, as long as his wife did not try to straighten up. He began to type.

In this world, Cali had established himself as a writer of fantasy. Fantasy they called it! Only if they knew how real it was. Dragons, mystics, spells, crystal balls, and wars. He remembered the battle in the universe of the three suns. Uomo. Linea. Cali loved Linea so… The power Linea held emanated from her love of the world around her; her sense of right and wrong. How could Uomo ever know that? Linea was bullheaded as Uomo. He wanted her power, she wanted to be left alone with it. Of course the energy suppressed in her unconscious mind revealed itself only when threatened. Someday she will know. When the time was right. Only in her dreams did she know her of travels, knowledge, danger. But to her, these were just dreams. Each time they fought Uomo, Linea forgot all through the time portal. And the trances caused by Uomo gave Linea the power to defeat him and give she and Cali new lives in new times.

Cali knew Uomo found them again. This time it would be different and Cali was afraid. Afraid for Linea; afraid to leave her – the dark mystic close. Far out at the edge of Andromeda, a black hole was forming in the future death of a star. It still would be many years before its full strength.

In the corner of the study, on a pedestal, the orb emanated a faint glow that was steadily getting brighter.

He kept typing.

Not fantasy at all.

Linea buzzed for her secretary, Miss Stevens, as she went through her file cabinets for papers and stuffed them into her attaché. Miss Stevens comes in the office with Linea's messages.

"Good morning, Mrs. Crown. I'm glad you're here."

"Why?" she read her messages and glances over her mail, "I hope it's nothing really pressing. I'm going right back home to work from there. Forward only the real important calls there. Reschedule my meetings and appointments."

"There's a gentleman waiting for you…"

"Does he have an appointment?"

"Nope."

"Well," Linea said grabbing her attaché and standing, "make sure he gets one next week."

"He said he wouldn't leave until he talked to you."

"If he gets tiresome, call security."

"And what would they do?" A tall man entered the room. He was Black-skinned, powerfully well built and extremely handsome.

Miss Stevens began to show her irritation. The man only smiled sweetly at her. Linea closed her file drawers, tucked her attaché under her desk and sat down.

"It's alright. I'll see him since he's here."

He said, "Thank you." Miss Stevens rolled her eyes at him and left the office.

Linea motioned for him to sit in one of the chocolate hued leather chairs in front of her mahogany desk, "You're an arrogant S.O.B."

"Thank you again."

"What can I do for you, Mr. …?"

"Uomo DiNero, Mrs. Crown. I need someone to help me with my career and manage my money. You were highly recommended."

"Uh huh, by whom?"

"Your rivals."

Linea laughed, "You act, Mr. DiNero?"

"All the time."

"I see." Linea watched him as he rattled off his credits, handing her his resume and photographs. She knew all about him already. Uomo DiNero was a good actor, but he was type cast. He did many Indie and cable films and music videos. An actor couldn't really fully cross over into mainstream films unless he looked like Will Smith, Vin Diesel or The Rock. Uomo's skin was the color of coal and all visible hair was a shocking white. There was a huge gold snake shaped ring on his index finger. Linea thought it was gaudy.

"You do have potential. Unfortunately you will be type cast for a little while longer until we get you better established." Linea pressed her intercom for her secretary, "We're going to set up some appointments for you. Be prompt and don't be argumentative. If you don't like something, you call me. I'll handle it. Understand?"

She handed him a business card as Miss Stevens walked in with papers.

"I'll go over the contracts with you. Miss Stevens, please call my husband for me."

"Sure," she turned and left again.

Uomo's heart turned angry, but he said nonchalantly, "Married. Too bad."

"For you," Linea shot back and continued to inform him the contents of his contract with her. "Now, Mr. DiNero, read this carefully. Ask me questions. Sign where you see the flags."

Miss Stevens' voice came over the intercom indicating Linea's call had been made and holding.

"Thank you," Linea said picking up her hand set, "Hey, baby. Yeah, new client. I won't be long. Bye."

All the while Uomo watches her lips as they move the words into the receiver, her eyes as she looks at her watch, her delicate fingers as they interweave in her long curly hair from the root to the ends pushing the course mane from her face as he writes his name over and over again.

When Linea placed the phone back in its cradle, Uomo handed her the papers.

"I hope you read these," she said

"I did."

Linea held out her hand to shake his. Uomo looked at it in awe, then gently it engulfed in his large palm. His hand seemed to seer her skin.

"Well, Mr. DiNero, your life, your professional life, all of it, is now in our hands. Don't worry we'll take very good care of you."

"I hope so."

"I know you're good. I've seen you before. I like your work, your spoiled brat attitude, we can play on that. Just don't play on it with me. Be straight with me and we'll do fine. Let's start with a more flattering haircut…"

She went on about his appointments. Possible screen tests for four parts. Uomo sat quietly, gazing at her intently. After all these years. He thought, a moment where he was not the enemy outright. She sat unafraid, not threatened by him. Talking to him. Smiling and complimenting him. Uomo began to feel… Feel what? Strong, confident and humbled by her.

Linea brought him back, "You alright? You look lost in thought."

His smile was warm, "No, I'm fine. It's just, um, nice to talk to someone who understands."

"It's not hard to understand what someone wants. That is why you came to me, isn't it, to get what you want? Let me make this perfectly clear that I will not do all the work. You are the one who is out there and you are the one who has to make this happen."

Uomo knew what she meant, but he couldn't help thinking about the meaning he wanted. Only to have her without fighting for her after all the fighting for her.

Miss Stevens walked in, handed Linea a small book and retreated again.

"OK, this is your appointment book. My number is already printed inside. Your full day with us begins tomorrow early. At five thirty you get a full makeover: facial, haircut, manicure, pedicure, blah, blah, blah. You going to have a new portfolio shot and printed to be ready for your screen test at one. At your makeover, they will be taking measurements and calling ahead to the photographer so her people can have your wardrobe ready. Now go home and get some rest."

Uomo stood and turned. Linea reached under her desk to retrieve her attaché and handbag, getting ready to leave herself. Half way across the office, he turned back to her.

"When do I see you again?"

Linea smiled, "Check your appointment book."

Cali was on a streak when Linea came in. She didn't disturb him and prepared lunch, listening to the keys of his keyboard click at a quick and steady pace. Not until she heard the tapping slow down did she greet him.

"Lunch is ready," she leaned against one of the many bookcases in his office.

He looked up, "I'm sorry, baby. I didn't hear you come in. Won't ask how long you been here."

"Good. Just come and eat." He sighed, saved the current work in progress and followed her into the kitchen.

"I'm sorry I couldn't get back right away like I planned. A new client made such a fuss with Stevens, so I saw him."

"One of those, huh?" They sat at the kitchen table and he served.

"Well, he's spoiled. He has the talent anyway to be that way."

"What's his name?" Cali knew the answer already.

"Uomo DiNero. You've seen his stuff. I have a hunch he'll be large."

"I always trust your hunches."

"I do, too. I did with you."

He smiled. Time was almost near. It was funny, a calm suddenly flowed through him.

# THREE YEARS LATER – AUTUMN

Uomo DiNero became a huge success as an actor in this world. His knack for ultimate drama and theatrics gained him a large cult following. As his salary increased each time he was in film, television or video, Linea's agency made sure they did right by him: he didn't squander his money on frivolous items or women. The agency was lucky that he didn't have an entourage. Uomo lavished gifts on Linea, gifts she always returned. Not by Cali's urging, but Linea's principles. And she made sure their relationship stayed on formal terms, though now they used their first names.

When Linea visited Uomo's filming strange occurrences happened when she was too near certain electrical equipment. Stage lights became brighter, light meters did not get correct readings, and film was overexposed when developed. Days she wasn't on the set, all was normal. Crews called her 'the jinx'.

Uomo was amused. He constantly teased Linea. Until she told him it would be economical for her not to be on the sets and stages. They were spending too much money to do retakes and replace equipment. The actor was annoyed, but saw she was right saving the producers time and money.

Between gigs, Uomo read Cali's novels. All he was doing was reading the chronicles of their past 'adventures'. Linea, Cali and his. Except for one; the last. It gave him high hope and dread deep in his heart.

He met with Linea a few weeks after he finished reading Cali's most current tale. He wanted to make a proposal over lunch instead in her office.

"Linea, I want to do a movie on one of your husband's books." He looked serious. Linea only smiled.

"You know Uomo, that's the first time you ever mentioned my husband for any reason." She leaned back in her chair and gazed at him. "OK. What's so special about it?"

He leaned forward, contemplating the food on his plate, "I don't know, but I like it. You know how I like sci-fi and this novel, his latest book, really moves me." He moved to touch her hand. Her experience with his touches made Linea discretely move before he reached her.

"I thought I'd, dare I say it, cry when the heroine died."

"What, not you, Uomo DiNero. I don't believe you."

He didn't know what to say to make her believe, "Please, Linea. I want to do this. I want to play the part of that reluctant conqueror, an antihero. You know it's what I do best."

Linea looked at the man across from her who did play the champion role so well. Roles an audience loved him and hated him in. He's asked very little from her. *Why not*, she thought.

"If Cali doesn't give rights, then that's it."

"Absolutely, Linea," he quietly turned his attention to his lunch. "You know I think of you constantly, Linea. I'm glad we're friends. In fact, I think you're the only friend I have."

"I'm flattered, Uomo, and pleased."

He glances up and Uomo's gaze holds hers; his eyes flash. For a moment Linea is mesmerized. She sees something that only Cali…

Cali! She looks at her watch, "Oh, Uomo. I hate to cut this short. I'm sorry. I've got to run. I'll call you later."

He only watches her dash away. Uomo sulks. Did she see him? After all these eons, for the first time, Uomo felt that was finally bequeathed to him could belong to him and him only.

*Cali must go*, he thought, *but it must not be by my hand. Or Linea will also die.*

And that must not come to pass.

Cali blinked, trying to relieve the glare from his eyes. The crystal flashed the entire room with its radiance, then deadened.

This was something new!

He reached for the crystal. Linea's image appeared as she made her appointment. She was walking away from Uomo. Uomo was brooding. Cali saw what he felt and there was that something new. Two men fighting for the power of one woman. The soul and body quickly follow when the heart leads. Uomo is on the right track. Love is something he has no control over – not even within himself.

Well, Linea was on her way home. Cali straightened up his desk and walked into the kitchen to prepare dinner.

The car's top folded back neatly. Linea zoomed through traffic. She laughed as the wind whipped her hair about her head. The red BMW seemed to fly beneath her. A feeling that thrilled her. Besides the fact that Linea loved to drive hard and fast, she was also late. There were a few things Linea had to pick up for Cali.

She loved Cali. Though she was very independent, Linea could not live without him. Today, she would surprise her husband armed with champagne and goodies to tell him about Uomo's request. Cali was so indifferent about things like that. He just loved to write. He didn't really care what other people thought; he was lucky their opinion was positive. Cali loved his writing and that's all that mattered.

Dinner's aroma met Linea at the door. Cali was not in the kitchen. She dropped her attaché on the counter. The ice bucket was already filled, so Linea placed the champagne in it, and with it grabbed two glasses to find Cali.

The courtyard, loaded with flowers, was where she found him setting the table.

"Baby, this is beautiful!" she blurted out.

"Thanks. I thought it would be nice out here for dinner. We can watch the sunset and the moon rise all at once. I checked the almanac."

"Awesome," she breathed in the bouquets' fragrance, reaching for a card attached to the flowers. “Aw, Cali, these aren’t from you and not to me. These are for you.”

“No kidding. They’re from Uomo. What’s the occasion that *he* sends *me* flowers?” He pulls out a chair for her.

Linea sighed, “Let’s eat, Cali, and I’ll tell you all about it. I’m starved.”

He kissed her on her neck; her scent made him feel better. “Uh oh, you bought champagne. You guys are up to something. Tell me or I won’t be able to eat.”

She laughed, “You pour, I’ll serve. Well, Uomo read your current bestseller and really loved it. He would like your permission to have a screenplay adaptation written. And he star in the movie.”

Linea looked up through her lashes at Cali. There on his face was a brief expression of disbelief; she had to look at him fully to see if she weren’t imagining it. A little smile appeared on his face instead. He popped the cork and began pouring.

“Are you serious? Is he really? A movie script?”

“Yes, yes, yes. He said he was moved to tears when the heroine died. Oh, he seemed so sincere. Uomo DiNero wants to do the movie.”

It was Cali’s turn to laugh, “Sure. Why not? I would like to see at least one of my novels made into a movie.”

"Are you sure, baby?"

He chewed slowly on the grilled salmon, though it was melting in his mouth, "Yes. This should be fun."

"Cheers, then, to a successful film," she raised her glass in a toast.

"Cheers, my love."

Later that night, Cali walked through their home aware of Linea's every movement though she was upstairs in the bedroom at the rear of the house. The flowers' pretty scent on the courtyard drew him outside. He sat crossed-legged on the manicured lawn in the darkness and meditated. One by one his muscles relaxed and he felt the energy surge.

For once he did not know what was going to happen and so much had to be done. He could foresee nothing. Above his upturned palms the orb formed. It did not glow – no danger. Cali dropped his hands and the orb dissolved. He looked around then stood up. Again, he looked around at the flowers and bowed.

"Thank you, Uomo. The legacy will be passed on. Thank you," he whispered to his floral audience. Cali quietly returned to sleep by Linea's side.

Cali awoke alone in bed. Linea had already gone to work. He looked over at the clock. It read ten thirty five. It was late! On the bathroom mirror was Linea's note: *Didn't want to wake you. You looked too peaceful. Call you later. Love you.*

He showered and dressed. With no words flowing in his mind, Cali decided a change for the day may do him some good. He decided to work in the garden, leaving the computer on just in case.

Half the day had gone by. There still was no flow. The laptop screen remained blank. Cali wanted Linea. Pushing himself away from the table, he finally logged off. As the familiar tones and beeps of the machine turning off were heard, the phone rang.

"Hi, babe." Linea's cheerful voice soothed him.

"Hey. I hope you're coming home early. I need you. Right now."

She purred, "Oooh, I know what you mean. Okay, listen, I'll be home in two hours. Let me finish my work. Want anything for me to bring home?"

"Why, yes, there is this little pink delicate thing I have a taste for..."

"I'll be there in one hour."

"Okay," and he hung up.

Uomo watched Linea as she spoke to Cali. He tried to control his jealousy and contempt for *him* at times like this. If he just grabbed her to wrap her in his arms and kiss her… No, that would not work. It never had before. He had to win Linea on her terms. He wanted to touch her, kiss her, make love to her. No, ravage her – his passion may not allow him to be subtle. Thoughts of Linea overwhelmed his very being.

And she belonged to Cali. Linea's love for him oozed from her. Uomo's eyes captured her eyes, lips, a peek of her breast, her legs, her long graceful fingers. Uomo stood up and clenched his fists into his pockets and turned away. He had to be patient.

"So, Uomo," she hung up the phone. He quickly returned to the chair in front of her desk. Her sexy eyes gazed lazily through him. "Who will we have write the script version of Cali's novel?"

He swallowed; Uomo felt timid before her. Lately, he was inept when they were alone.

"I would like to do it. I can keep it close to his original ideas since I have a passion and obligation to Cali for giving me this honor."

"Passion and obligation, huh? What will you do? Go off somewhere and write?"

"Precisely. I'll tell you what: if Cali doesn't like it, I'll get one of the best sci-fi screenwriters in the business. I'll pay him myself."

Linea thought a few minutes, tapping an enameled fingernail slowly on the desk.

"Okay," she picked up Uomo's copy of the thumb-nailed and worn hardcover novel and flipped through to the last page of the book. Five hundred twenty seven pages. She gently laid it on her desk.

"How much time do you think you'll need, Uomo?" she asked him as her palm flattened down against the cover of the book.

He scratched his head and shrugged, "A month, maybe two tops."

"Really?" She pushed the book across her desk towards him, "You got enough supplies to do what you have to do?"

"Yes."

"Get to work. I'll call you next week to see how you're doing."

His eyes flashed as he grinned. Uomo grabbed up the book, he hopped out of his chair and he was out the door. Linea buzzed her secretary. She began straightening up her desk and packed her attaché.

"You rang?" Miss Stevens was at the door smiling.

"Yes. I'll be working from home the next couple of days. Please finish up here and put the machine on. I'm giving you a few days paid vacation. I'll see you on Monday."

"Thank you, Mrs. Crown."

"Thank *you.* It's been a good year for this agency."

It took three weeks for Uomo to complete a first draft of the script, working day and night. His appearance was ragged. With no sleep or exercise he looked slim and gray. After the first three or four days of reading and re-reading Cali's novel to absorb every nuance and feeling, Uomo sat at his computer and never got up.

He didn't change a thing from the original text and there were very few cuts. The integration may have been his, but the story didn't waver. Uomo hoped Cali would approve. Approval from Cali – it was a very strange thing for Uomo.

This would be the beginning of the end. The end of everything and Uomo was afraid.

Miss Stevens buzzed in, interrupting Linea's meeting with another client, "I'm sorry, but Mr. DiNero is here to see you."

Linea spoke softly into the receiver, "How is he?"

"He looks awful," was the secretary's answer.

"Order a big lunch for him from Fratelli's with lots of fruit and vegetable wraps. They know Uomo. Tell them it's for him. They'll know what to bring. Put Uomo in one of the private rooms so he can lie down. I'll be out as soon as I'm done here. Thank you."

Linea hung up the phone, "I'm sorry, Laura. Tell me how the screen test with Spielberg went…"

She listened, but did not entirely hear all the news. Her attention was toward Uomo in the other room. It was as though Linea could feel Uomo's movements, the exhaustion in his very being and the satisfaction and anxiety of the finished script he held in his arms. She felt him lie down and stretch out on a sofa, then nothing. Linea's brain registered Laura's excitement and heard her. The agent gave her client a few more appointments to keep and escorted her out of her office. Miss Stevens made sure she left the building. They turned to each other.

"Is anyone else scheduled today?" Linea asked.

“No,” Miss Stevens answered, “Mr. DiNero is in the blue room.”

“Did he eat anything?” Miss Stevens shook her head. They started toward the direction of where their star client was. They were like two schoolgirls bearing a secret.

The blue room only contained three blue leather sofas and a huge table. It was used mostly for promotions of their artists. The main reason it was called the blue room was the wall-to-wall, floor-to-ceiling window that framed the best Manhattan skyline view in Brooklyn.

The table was set with food. Linea looked it over to see if Uomo picked over anything. He didn’t. Miss Stevens stayed at the door awaiting instructions. She watched as her boss picked up a piece of sliced pear and chew it, deep in thought. Linea walked over to Uomo and studied him. He was stretched out, one arm behind his head, the other holding the script across his chest. His long frame over-extended the sofa; his feet propped up upon the cushioned arm. Around his eyes were puffy and cheeks slightly sunken. He was clean and dressed in a tailored white shirt, blue jeans and cowboy boots. Miss Stevens closed the door as she left the area.

Linea stood over Uomo. His face was peaceful, though his eyes stirred rapidly under their lids.

She touched his hand, “Uomo.” His hand was hot but bearable. He breathed deeply and his eyes blinking open. For a moment his dark eyes were crystal clear, then their color returned. Linea wasn’t sure what she saw, but she knew she did. She said nothing.

“Was I out long?” Uomo yawned.

“About an hour. Hungry?” Linea said.

“Famished,” he left the script where he lain and went to the table. As he fixed himself a plate piled high with vegetable wraps and fruit, Linea picked up the script.

“May I?”

Uomo glanced over his shoulder, nodded. He began to eat looking over the cityscape. Linea sat, flipping the pages; she only glanced over the storyline. But when she began reading intently as if the story drew her in, the images were vivid in her mind, even for a script.

“What page are you on?” Uomo asked standing near her, studying her.

Startled, Linea looked up at him. He smiled.

“You have something smeared on your face,” she glanced at the page number as he wiped his mouth, “I read forty pages! This is amazing, Uomo. Is it alright now if I take this to Cali?”

“That’s who it’s for.”

Linea dropped off Uomo and headed home herself. Cali was waiting for her on the front step. He looked into her eyes; he knew yet he was not excited. He sensed her anticipation.

"Cali, it's good," she was grinning.

"Dinner's ready" is all he said, taking the bound papers from her. His novel was tucked under one arm.

"Have you eaten, baby?" She knew that he would want to be alone until he was finished.

"Yes," he kissed her. She knew he hadn't. "I'll be in my office."

He led her into their home, closed the door and left her in the foyer. When she entered the dining room, the table was set. Forcing down her meal, Linea's anxiety took away her appetite. She washed the dishes and cleaned the kitchen. Her conscience had to be clear for her to do paperwork. The script kept entering her mind. After a while, the only thing she could do was go to bed.

When the sun rose, Cali still hadn't been to bed. Linea sleepily walked down the stairs and into the kitchen. Frozen air hit her skin when she opened the refrigerator door. She didn't realize she was naked. Cali came up behind her as she reached for the water pitcher. They made love on the kitchen floor.

A large grin covered Linea's face as she got on the phone, "Steve, I got a something here that will knock *Star Wars* on its butt."

Cali stood near holding the script close to his heart.

There were very few changes in the final draft. Producers were effortlessly pulling money in to fund the film. It was all for the perfect novel adaptation. All the best special effects people were called. Costumes were made by a top designer. Several states put in bids for the sets to be in their areas. Within months, filming began.

Cali and Linea never set foot on the sets, though the director wanted Cali's input. Cali only told them to go for what Uomo thought best; the script was great.

The movie was ahead of schedule, which pleased everyone. Especially Uomo. Uomo radiated a powerful presence on the sites; most takes were shot under three times. His co-stars followed him and found his advice outstandingly useful. Everything went smoothly. By the time the film reached the editing room, the techs couldn't select what takes should be in the final cut.

Uomo took a long vacation. Actually, he disappeared. Linea left phone messages for him to come for a small dinner celebration after the premiere with the crews, producers, the music people and the director. There were promotional pictures to be taken and rounds to the talk shows, daytime, news and night talk show hosts were requesting him to appear on their shows.

Uomo was not to be found. It was the perfect publicity stunt.

The critics applauded the movie.

The media praised the film on its adaptation from the novel they all read written by a writer they all loved to read.

The entertainment section in all the papers released carried the lead story and stock photographs of Cali Crown with his lovely wife, and Uomo's manager, Linea. The first weekend the film was released grossed over one hundred million dollars, the greatest amount in history for one film released on a weekend – and it stayed number one for the longest amount of time.

Uomo won an Oscar for his film script adaptation of a novel. He didn't want best actor; knew he wouldn't get it anyway. What he won was deeply satisfying. He accepted the statuette via satellite; no one still knew where he was. And no one could tell where he was – the background of his location was black. Cali shyly accepted the award for Uomo and held up the prize up to the camera for the star to see.

Cali was dead.

One morning he couldn't catch his breath. Linea came out of the shower and he was at the edge of the bed gasping weakly. She ran to him.

"Cali, Cali! What's wrong? What's happened?"

He wheezed, "Can't breathe."

Linea quickly called 9-1-1, "Don't fight it, Cali. Just breathe, please just relax and take breaths. Cali, please!"

She watched him die. He lay in her arms until the ambulance came. The police were actually first because they knew it was the home of celebrities. They had to break the door in. Linea was giving CPR to her already blue tinged husband. Tears streaming down her beautiful face as she fought for her husband's life. They coaxed her into letting him go when the paramedics finally arrived moments later. She kissed Cali for the last time then they laid him on the bed.

She whispered, "He just stopped breathing…"

Pneumonia was the cause of death. The atmosphere in this time destroyed his body. Cali was not immune to the impurities of a modern world. Uomo was elated. But the feeling hastily vanished when he finally reappeared weeks later and saw Linea.

She took bereavement leave, then sick leave, and finally never showed up to work. Linea didn't see or talk to anyone, not even Miss Stevens. Newspapers ran four to five page spreads on Cali Crown's life and accomplishments and magazines dedicated entire issues to Cali and his novels and all the people ever involved with him. Cali Crown novels were hot commodities and no bookstores, brick and mortar nor online, could keep copies of anything he wrote. Linea mourned terribly; Uomo knew it but could not find her lifelight. He contacted her attorneys who had not been able to contact her, nor Cali's publishers nor the movie company.

Uomo feared the worst.

The Crown house was dark. Uomo stayed in his car, it seemed for hours, watching. There was no noise or movement. He hesitantly got out of his car. He felt something strange. He circled to the back of the home, peeking in the windows. Linea was in the den and there was an eerie glow from the corner of the room out of his sight and her back was to them both. She seemed to be reading. Uomo was puzzled; the room was pitch black, except for that faint glow in the corner. He tapped lightly on the window as to not startle her. Linea slowly turned and it was he that was taken aback! Her eyes were glowing.

"Linea?" he called out to her, wondering if she had found her meaning, the meaning of it all in the power. But as she walked toward the window, closer and closer, the luminosity faded from her eyes as well as in the corner. She was wearing a floor length lace gown; it clung to her. And her long hair was simply combed back out of her face. She looked more beautiful to Uomo as she ever did. Opening the window, Linea smiled meekly at Uomo.

"Back door is open." She was looking right through him.

She still had not turned on any lights and when the kitchen light flickered on Uomo had to take a few seconds to adjust. She was suddenly in front of him staring at him questionably.

Uomo took her hands, "I am so sorry, Linea." She didn't pull away from him and the heat of her shocked him. "Are you well?"

"Yes, thanks, Uomo. I'm really glad you came by. I wanted to talk to someone." She turned from him. "I was going to make something to eat. Would you like to…join me?"

It sounded to him she was just making conversation, "Yes, I'd like that. But let me cook you something. It's the least I can do. OK?"

Her back was still turned, "Yes. That's fine."

"Are you sure you are alright?"

"Yes."

He opened the refrigerator. It was full. Uomo turned back to take a good look at Linea. She had become thinner, but fuller somehow.

"Uomo, I lost my baby a couple of weeks back," Linea said as if she read his thoughts, "I called my doctor to come here, a doctor I trusted. I didn't want anyone to know. You know how the press is. After that, I didn't know what to do."

"Linea…"

"No," she faced him, "I stopped crying already. I'm fine. Physically, anyway."

Now he saw it: her breasts and hips were full, but her ribcage was prominent and her cheeks were sunken in. She hadn't been eating or sleeping. He prepared her a large, nutritious meal and made her eat as much as possible. She talked the whole time.

"I want to sell the house and all the furniture. I can't stay here or amongst these things we shared. I'll just take his books; they're all first editions." She paused to chew thoughtfully, "You know, I've reread everything he's written and I found some other papers I don't know what to do with right now. I think eventually I'll let his publishers see them. They've asked if he'd written anything prior, and he has. He had just completed a manuscript and it's very good. *Very* good."

She pushed away her plate of barely touched braised filet of sole, salad greens and sweet potatoes. "I miss him dreadfully."

He pushed the plate back, "Just take a few more bites, Linea. I'm going to take care of you from now on. Now, eat."

"OK, OK."

Uomo was true to his word.

Linea returned to her former self and began working again. She sold the house privately. Buying another in Virginia furnished with only Cali's writings placed carefully in the bookcases in her private library off the bedroom, the ancient orb and her clothing.

Uomo made frequent visits to see her. They became close friends, though Uomo still felt closed out from her. They made trips together, mostly to his shoots, where her electromagnetic jinx dissipated. Rumors spread that they were lovers, when they were seen together in various parts of the world. She stopped traveling with him. Uomo then would only work when Linea was well taken care of so he could leave her.

"Uomo, I don't need you. Don't you have a life of your own?" She asked him one day after he made such a fuss.

He took her in his arms tenderly for the first time, "Come here to me, Linea. My life is with you."

"Uomo, please…" she protested.

"I know you can't love me as you loved Cali, but I can't break from you. I, I love you. I always have. Could you accept me and love me? Marry me?"

Linea calmly looked up at him, "Go do your movie now, Uomo. I'll give you an answer when you're finished shooting."

But when shooting wrapped up and the film hit the editing room, Linea could not be found anywhere.

Uomo became frantic. For weeks he used every power he had in the cave deep down in the earth beneath his home searching for signs of her. Just when he was about to devastate the earth for her, Linea's lifelight was strong at his front door. She had returned as mysteriously as she had vanished. Linea had come to *him*.

He opened the front door and he was terrified and angry.

"I was afraid that you weren't home. Did you miss me, Mo?" Then she smiled that beautiful smile. Uomo wasn't angry any longer. He grabbed her up into his arms and kissed her, "I thought I lost you again."

Her tears mingled with his, "No, never."

They were married the next day.

Uomo bought a villa on a small island off the coast of Spain nearest Africa. He gave it to Linea as a wedding gift. The island had its own landing strip. The main industry on the island was cotton that was harvested and woven into cloth by the inhabitants, dyed naturally into batik patterns. A caretaker took care of everything for them.

An awkward feeling loomed over Linea and Uomo. After a large and untouched meal was prepared for them, the staff was dismissed for the evening. A light tropical rain began. Linea sat quietly on a lounge in the master bedroom looking out into the twilight with a brush in her hand. The spectacular golden red sunset submerged behind the distant mountains. The couple was dressed in their nightclothes: Uomo in magenta and gold batik satin pants and a plain white island logo t-shirt. Linea wore a slinky blue gown. Uomo watched her every move as she brushed her hair; he wondered what she was thinking.

Suddenly, she dropped the brush, rose from her position and walked out of the room, out of the villa into the fragrant gardens. Her new husband right behind.

In the rain, Linea stood with her arms outstretched, welcoming the refreshing shower. Uomo pulled off his top as Linea turned slowly around facing him, her eyes were closed letting the water hit her uplifted face and a smile graced her lips. He came closer to her placing his hands around her waist. Linea opened her eyes. Her hands rested on his powerful shoulders. Passion sparked between them. Uomo kissed her; their embrace tightened, the kiss deepened. He stopped to push her gown off her delicate shoulders. His hand slowly, lightly caressed her body. Kneeling in front of her, Uomo rested his head on her belly.

"I want to make you happy, Linea." Tremors shot through him as her fingers combed through his hair. He laid her on the wet grass. The heat of the damp earth steamed up around them. Their eyes spoke. Uomo tasted her body and lingered on the places where she moaned the loudest until she lost control. He kissed her again. Tasting herself on his sweet, hot tongue. His pants were tugged off, but Uomo hesitated. He was still afraid of what might happen. But they couldn't stop now. He looked down at her and placed his arm behind her neck. Linea long black hair was wet and her lips were parted, eyes lazily gazing up at him, waiting. Their skin was slippery. Uomo dared on. They gasped and moved together on the wet turf.

"Mo," she was barely audible. Uomo looked down at her and she was luminescent.

He entered her after what seemed like hours. She bit her lip with a moan. Her eyes fluttered.

At last, she gave herself to him, unyieldingly. Centuries of desire tempered his pace. Uomo realized he had been saving himself for her. His obsession to have Linea left no time for any other woman. Desire's tear's fell upon her face and blended with the rain.

"I was always meant for you, Linea," he whispered in her ear, "I have *never* loved another."

"Mo, I am yours."

She kissed him so deeply and held him so tightly he begins to feel his tormented soul lift from him. Her long legs wraps around his powerful ones. His passion climbs as her thrusts matches his. Uomo's body began to quake.

The feeling is too delicious for him to think, "What is happening to me?"

"You have become mortal, my love."

He was startled by her words; he knew her eyes were illuminated though they were closed. There was a smile on her face; he kissed her again. Linea's luscious body trembled under him, with him. Sounds of the creatures that roamed the garden at night became louder as Uomo rocked into her and she took all of him. *Being mortal feels exquisite*, he thought, *Exquisite!*

Then all his thoughts were no more.

"Would you like to do that again?" Linea's voice woke him from his trance. His skin was tingling; his muscles tight and ready to go again. Yes, oh yes.

"Woman, I don't think I can stop." He felt himself growing again. Uomo was no longer an enemy or lonely. He gave himself to her. The grounded god was pleased.

Miles away, the crystal orb flashed in a blinding light and imploded.

When the sun rose, Uomo carried his exhausted wife into the master bedroom, leaving their bedclothes in the garden. They didn't leave the room for two days. The servants were ignored.

"Newlyweds," the manservant grinned, when they didn't answer his knock on the door when he brought them their meals. "They'll come out when they're ready."

Uomo and Linea were rarely seen after their wedding. They sold their houses and bought a plantation in South America. They both retired from Hollywood disregarding the pleas from their associates. Eventually, people began to see that they were in love. Paparazzi of them in the rain forests never came out – a strange aura blotted their images out. But reports surface that they always looked happy.

On a visit to New York, Linea stopped by Cali's publishing house, telling them about the new manuscript. They were ecstatic. She made a deal, promising to send the novel as soon as she returned home and left their offices.

Uomo and Linea were unheard from for three years.

"Taylor!"

The German Sheppard raced to his mistress and sat in front of her at attention, his ears pointed high. Linea hugged the loyal animal.

"Get Mo."

She let the dog dash off. Linea had some news for Uomo. Since they were married, Uomo and Linea stayed in seclusion. Not wanting to be disturbed by anyone, they kept within the various estates they owned. They raised horses and dogs. Uomo was attentive and loving and he knew that Linea gave Uomo her all – though deep inside Uomo felt Cali was still in her mind. Cali was still somewhere.

Somewhere nearby.

Uomo watched Taylor bound toward the stables. He didn't become alarmed because it was nearly lunchtime, the dog usually came to fetch him around this time. The crew broke for lunch. Uomo raced the dog home.

When Uomo showered and looked for Linea, he found her in the gazebo with a large lunch. Champagne was chilled. She was quietly fanning herself in the double swing. Linea grew more beautiful each time her husband saw her. Uomo came to the conclusion millennia before that he had to have her. The battles he and Cali had to win her, her power. Now, Linea had Uomo instead of him possessing her. Nights, he couldn't sleep without touching or holding her.

He often wondered if he were ever really immortal.

"What's the occasion?"

"Sit down, Mo, and I'll serve." Linea popped the champagne, the best from their cellar, and served his lunch. He sees she didn't pour champagne for herself. They ate quietly. Uomo wanted to know what was on her mind. He waited patiently.

Finally she said, "I got a call from my doctor."

Alarm. "Your doctor? Are you alright?"

"Oh, yes," she laughed, "I'm pregnant."

"What!?"

"Didn't you think it was bound to happen? Mo, we make love all the time. I haven't menstruated in five months."

He looked at her for several moments, her words absorbing, and slowly smiled remembering their coupling; he literally unloaded all he had into her each time. It always felt too good. Uomo knelt in front of her and laid his hand on Linea's growing abdomen.

"I love you, Linea. I've never been so happy."

It had been twelve hours since the first excruciating contraction. Linea was having a terrible delivery. The doctor had told the parents they were expecting twins. Uomo heard Linea's screams and moans. It shattered his nerves. People were scurrying in and out from the birthing room. He couldn't take it. Uomo covered his eyes. Several moments passed. A high-pitched scream pierced his eardrums. He slowly realized it was the same scream back in the cave…

Uomo dashed into the room Linea was giving birth. Her attendants were still as stone. He became afraid. The doctor and nurses were in suspended animation. Time had stopped. There was a glow emanating from the bed where Linea lay.

He stepped closer. An aura surrounded her. It was bright and strong. Lifelight. Above her, the twins levitated. They were crying wholeheartedly. The healthier their cry the more their auras glowed, and Linea's weaker.

"Uomo."

Linea reached out for him and took his hands, "I will live only a short time longer and I must tell you what must be done. My purpose is complete."

His voice almost would not leave his throat, "No, no. Linea! You cannot leave me. Not now, not ever."

"I will not leave you ever. Behold, your children. They are your destiny now."

He looked at them barely seeing them through his tears. Daughters. His daughters. They were mirror images of Linea gazing back at him and smiling her smile.

"You will have each other. You must deliver them to their husbands as Cali brought me to you."

"Cali…" Cali's passing brought Uomo and Linea together. It was, in the end, certain.

"I was to be yours when the time was right. Not before. You, Uomo, were not patient. We have become mortal, but for a short time, to continue our immortality. Our daughters continue where I leave off."

Uomo shook his head over and over, repeating, "No, no. This is unbearable."

"Listen to me, Uomo: Cali's last manuscript is your map and instructions."

Uomo protested still, "Does it not matter that I love you? To finally know what love is. To be together, you and I, after all these eons?"

"Oh yes, it matters. When you have done your duty for these girls, we will be together again. I will come for you."

Tears slipped from his crystal clear eyes. Uomo held Linea close. Her aura dimmed.

"I love you Uomo. I'll be waiting…"

Time and light returned. The doctor and nurses moved. The nurses held the babies as they watched their father weep openly. These infants held their mother's knowledge and power within them. They understood. The doctor led everyone out of the room.

They were alone. Uomo was alone. He laid Linea straight, her arms resting at her sides, palms up. Uomo stood at the foot of their bed. His arms raised outward.

"Free!" he cried. From Linea's body was a blinding light. An apparition pulled from her body and floated above. It was she. She smiled, and then the apparition formed into a sphere that then crystallized. Uomo took hold of the sphere lovingly and left.

The girls were sleeping. They were in separate basinets. It would be a long task before he met Linea again. Without her, Uomo feared he may go mad.

He named them Merle and Aurora. Night and day. Uomo waited until the twins were eight years old before he taught them the ways of manipulating time and light. They were fourteen before they fully understood what they must do. They were skilled with their powers. Merle used her power secretly, usually when she was in trouble, and Aurora had rather not use her power at all. They grew beautiful, strong and cunning. And mighty.

Late one evening, the crystal appeared in their bedroom. They then transported themselves into their father's cave. He wore his black cloak. The crystal went to him. Uomo place it gently in a leather pouch along with Cali's manuscript. He looked at them. They were Linea doubled in front of him. His heart was in pain of her memory. And now, he was a protector. A legacy. Merle and Aurora just turned eighteen. There were many exceptionally powerful lifelights searching for them. Searching for his children. It was not time for them to have suitors and any and all will incur the wrath of Uomo before they marry his daughters.

"It is time, my daughters."

He gestured with his right finger. The gaudy snake ring grinned. They went to him, their eyes glowing bright. Three auras consumed them. They traveled to another time, another light, to find the balance of the meaning of everything. Through the black hole at the edge of a distant galaxy they went. Time shift.

This is only the beginning. Again.

www.ingramcontent.com/pod-product-compliance
Ingram Content Group UK Ltd.
Pitfield, Milton Keynes, MK11 3LW, UK
UKHW020218250726
13967UKWH00001B/73

9 780557 744534